An Older Man Bundle

Kristianna Sawyer et al.

Published by Publishers' Portal, 2016.

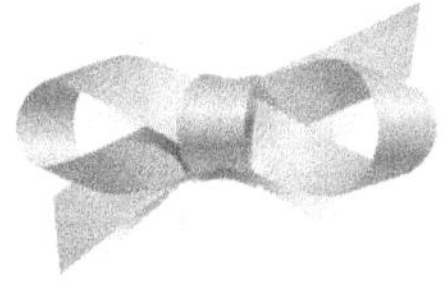

Erin's Unexpected Lover

ON THE NIGHT ERIN DECIDES to give in to her boyfriend's increasingly pressured demands for sex, she discovers Chip has already moved on. Devastated by his cheating, she finds sympathy in an unlikely person—Chip's father. Jared comforts Erin, but his soothing caresses change to something more. She will lose her virginity as planned, but to an unexpected lover in an all-consuming tide of passion that allows no room for thinking about little things like condoms or consequences...

Chapter One

"You're just being selfish."

"No, I'm just not ready yet, Chip. I want it to be special."

He scoffed. "I'm not special enough for you? It hurts my feelings, makes me think you don't trust me, when you tell me no all the time."

She wrung her hands, frustrated and overwhelmed. "I do trust you, Chip, but you can't expect me to have sex with you in the backseat of your car."

"Fine, then don't." He sat up and clambered back over to the front seat, not waiting for her to right her clothes or even sit up fully in the back and put on a seatbelt before turning on the engine and peeling out of the lookout point's parking lot. A few minutes later, he dropped her off at her house. "You can't expect me to wait forever, Erin. A man has needs." Then he drove off with a squeal of tires against the road.

That had been two nights ago, and Erin couldn't help reliving the fight over and over in her mind as she drove across town to the Maxwell residence, where Chip lived with his father. She had done some hard thinking and finally decided she was holding back on sex because she was afraid of it hurting. Chip cared about her, and he would do his best to make it not hurt. She might be a virgin at nineteen, but he was twenty and had already had several girlfriends, so he would know how to be a tender lover.

Erin hoped he wouldn't still be angry with her. She had gone to a lot of trouble to prepare for him tonight, planning to surprise him with her surrender to his increasingly urgent requests for lovemaking. After two months, she supposed it was time, and it certainly wasn't unreasonable of him to expect their relationship to deepen. It was the next natural step, and she'd been silly about holding off so long.

Chip's dad owned the largest house in the area. The three-story home sprawled across the edge of a bluff overlooking the ocean. The place had tight security, and she used the badge Chip had recently given her to let herself in through the electronic gate. She drove her third-hand car up the winding drive, parking near the circular loop that ran around the front of the house.

Erin took a moment to flip open the mirror on her visor and assess her appearance. She'd curled her hair and left it floating free in a cloud of amber-brown that framed her heart-shaped face and offset her tawny eyes. Makeup had subtly emphasized the shape of her lips and highlighted her cheekbones. Thankfully, her older sister knew a lot about beauty, working at a salon, and had assisted her with the evening's preparations.

After adjusting her breasts to better hide her nipples, she smoothed down the lime-green fabric as she got out of the car. The dress and matching platform heels were loaners from her sister, who was fully supportive of her decision to press ahead with giving Chip her virginity.

The clear platforms were hard to walk in, but she'd mostly mastered them by the time she climbed the marble stairs and reached the front door. The butler opened it a moment later, wearing a fierce frown.

That made Erin frown. She'd been to the house several times, and Mr. Edwin had always maintained a neutral expression, much like the sentinels at Buckingham Palace. To see him displeased was disconcerting. "Um, hello, Mr. Edwin."

After a second, his expression cleared, resuming its accustomed blandness. "Good evening, Ms. Pennibaker."

"I'm here to see Chip."

"Of course." With what appeared to be a deep sigh, he escorted her inside and waved up the stairs. "Master Maxwell is in his room, miss."

Feeling bemused by the butler's strange reaction, she made her way up two of the three flights of stairs. Chip's room was on the second floor, so she'd never had reason to venture to the top floor, where Jared Maxwell had his living quarters. His dad was a little intimidating, so she tended to shy away from his presence.

When she reached Chip's door, Erin thought about knocking, but hesitated. In her mind's eye, she pictured slipping inside, untying the two bows that kept the wrap-dress on, and letting it fall to her feet. He would be shocked, and pleased, to discover she wore nothing underneath.

Emboldened by his perceived reaction, Erin twisted the knob and opened the door quietly. She stepped past the doorjamb, hands on the bow at her side, but froze. A gasp escaped her, followed by a choked cry. She shook her head, wanting to deny what her eyes saw.

Chip was on his bed with a naked woman. His bare ass jiggled rhythmically as he plowed into his partner, who was cooing and calling his name in a squeaky voice that sounded a bit like a pigeon.

"Chip?" Even as she said his name, begging for some excuse, something to let her believe she wasn't seeing what she was, her heart shattered in her chest. The guilty way he froze, and then jumped off his partner, broadcast his actions just as clearly as the sight of him fucking her. "Oh, Chip."

"Erin?" He frowned, looking disconcerted for a moment, before his expression hardened. "What are you doing here?"

"I..." No way was she going to reveal what her plans had been. Plans that had withered and died in a second. "Oh, never mind, you bastard."

Tears scalded her eyes, and she wanted to turn and run from the room, but something kept her rooted to the spot.

Without making any attempt to hide his nudity, Chip shrugged, facing her fully with his still-hard cock waggling around. "What'd you expect? If you don't want to act like a woman, it's your fault I had to go elsewhere. I'm done playing virginal games with you, Erin."

"And I'm done with you." Erin's hands shook as she ripped off the necklace he'd given her a couple of weeks ago. It was the only thing she wore besides the dress and shoes. It cut into her neck a bit, but she didn't really notice the pain as the metal broke. With all her strength, she hurled it at the boy she had foolishly thought she loved and spun on her ridiculously high shoes.

Tears scalded her cheeks, and a sob broke free from her as she left his room, racing toward the stairwell. Her damned shoes picked that moment to fail her, and she went flying, landing hard on her butt. The pain of her tailbone colliding with the hardwood floor made her cry out, and new tears spilled from her. She wasn't even entirely sure if she was crying because of Chip's betrayal, the pain in her ass, or both.

"Erin, what's going on?"

She looked up at the sound of Jared's slightly stern voice above her. He loomed over her in a black silk robe that gaped open to display a generous expanse of her ex-boyfriend's father's chest. Erin averted her eyes and tried to stand up. To her surprise, Jared bent down to lift her into his arms.

She should protest and insist on walking, but it was nice to have warm arms holding her, offering her comfort, even if their owner didn't realize he was doing so. Erin buried her face against the silk of his robe, letting her tears soak into the expensive material.

He carried her up the stairs, but she didn't pay much attention to their surroundings until he lowered her onto a chaise lounge a few minutes later. As Jared sat beside her, she swiped at her cheeks and looked around, startled to find herself in what must be the older man's room. It was luxurious, but tasteful, and she briefly marveled that people lived like this every day.

He patted her back. "Tell me what's wrong, Erin."

No, his voice wasn't stern. That was just a natural note of authority, she realized. Nodding, she whispered, "I fell and hurt my bu...self."

"Poor girl." He frowned. "Surely not all this is because of a fall? And why wasn't Chip there to help you?"

She sniffled. "He's too busy with the girl in his room."

Jared's handsome features conformed into an expression of sympathy. "Oh, I'm so sorry." He rubbed her back in small circles. "My son is an idiot."

Erin shook her head. "It's my fault." Tears leaked from her eyes anew, and she bent forward, not hesitating to accept the shoulder he offered.

"How could it be your fault?" he asked, his voice rumbling through his chest against her ear.

"I wouldn't..." She sniffed again, trying to regain control. "I wasn't ready to sleep with him, so he found someone who would."

Jared cursed. "That idiot." He hugged her tightly. "I've always tried to teach Chip to go for substance over flash, but he has too much in common with his mother."

His words were a nice balm to her shaky self-esteem, but she was compelled to argue. Looking up, she met his gaze, unable to help noticing how soft his gray eyes were. "I shouldn't have been such a baby about it."

Jared frowned. "How old are you?"

"Nineteen."

He grimaced. "You have plenty of time yet, and there's no reason to rush into sex. Are you waiting for marriage?"

She shook her head.

"Religious reasons?"

Again, Erin shook her head.

He tapped her chest very gently with one finger, centered on her heart. "So, look in here and figure out why you weren't ready to have sex with Chip."

She wrinkled her brows, really thinking about it for a long time. "I guess I just didn't quite trust Chip." The admission embarrassed her, and she looked away, breaking eye contact with Jared. It was odd to admit she didn't trust his son, but that was the truth. In the back of her mind, she'd always half-expected Chip to return to his player ways. Of course, she'd been naïve enough to think he'd actually break up with her first.

A gentle hand on her chin forced her to look back at him. "That's good. You trusted your instincts."

Erin wiped at her face, suddenly conscious of just what a mess she must be. "I didn't completely. Tonight, I was going to sleep with him." She whispered the confession, licking her dry lips. Her gaze flew up when Jared moaned softly. "Are you okay?"

He nodded, but still looked a little pained. "Wait here." He got up, tightening the tie of his robe a bit, as he walked out of the room through another door. When he returned with a wet cloth, she assumed that room must be the bathroom.

Erin held out her hand for the washcloth, but he ignored it. Instead, Jared sat down beside her again, as close as before, and began cleaning her face with gentle strokes. After a few minutes, he nodded, looking satisfied. "That's much better, honey. You don't need all that junk anyway." His perfectly shaped lips formed a warm smile that made her stomach clench. "I personally prefer you in your usual state."

"Thank you, Mr. Maxwell." For some reason, his kindness triggered another round of tears, and she went back to his arms willingly, actively seeking out the comfort his body provided. His firm body. Jared was a warm, solid presence against her. With a little start, she realized the man holding her was quite muscular, and his skin was a welcome heat burning through the thin robe covering him.

She was embarrassed when her nipples suddenly tightened to hard little points. Erin lifted her head, searching his expression. "I, I think I'm okay now, Mr. Maxwell."

"Jared," he said in a throaty whisper.

She nodded, but didn't have the temerity to use his proffered first name. "Um, I should go now."

Jared cupped the back of her head, his thumb gently caressing the line of her jaw. "Maybe you should wait a few more minutes, to make sure you're composed. I couldn't bear it if you were in an accident because you left too soon."

"Okay." She licked her lips, watching the way his gaze followed the action. Her body tingled with the beginnings of arousal. "Thank you for being so kind. He's your son, so I'm surprised you didn't side with him."

Jared arched a brow. "He may be my son, but I'm well aware of his faults. My ex-wife has a taste for gaudy, flashy, easy crap, and Chip is just like her." His thumb continued stroking her face, and it was both soothing and arousing. "To lose a woman like you for some quick pussy is shortsighted, but he's young." Jared sighed. "Young people seldom realize the value of what they have."

Her face flushed bright red at his use of the word pussy, making her feel gauche and silly to find it startling. "You're very nice to me, Mr. Maxwell."

"Jared," he reminded.

"Jared," she said softly, getting a thrill from saying his name. "I'm glad I found out before I had sex with him," she said with a decisive nod.

"Absolutely. Your first time should be special, with someone who appreciates you." Imperceptibly, he drew her forward a bit, though still not touching her besides with his hand on her head, and the other hand on the middle of her back. "You're too beautiful and precious to waste on someone as shallow as Chip."

Forbidden thoughts were creeping into her mind, along with fierce, undeniable yearnings overtaking her body. Her nipples were harder than ever, and her slit throbbed with desire. Each swipe of his thumb across her jaw made her shiver. She knew Jared must be at least twenty years older than she was, but she was finding that less important with each minute that passed. Feeling the need to escape her own urges, she said, "I really need to go."

"I'll miss seeing you around here, Erin," he said with a hint of sadness. "It's become one of the highpoints of my day. Well, evening," he said with a chuckle. "I suffer from terrible insomnia and usually end up working most of the night and sleeping part of the day."

Which explained the robe. She suddenly wondered if he was wearing anything underneath it, or if he was as bare as she was in her thin dress? Could two layers of fabric be all that was separating their naked bodies? Cream dampened her pussy at the thought, and she shifted restlessly, inadvertently bringing herself closer to Jared.

Shyness and a tinge of fear urged her to stand up, and she struggled to her feet. Once again, the cursed shoes orchestrated her downfall, this time causing her to land squarely on his lap. Erin gasped as the hardness of his erection nestled against the wet heat of her folds. Her dress had been displaced during the fall, and only his black robe separated them.

His cheeks took on a ruddy hue. "I can't apologize for my reaction to your proximity, Erin, but I'm sorry if I've embarrassed you."

She blushed. He'd made no attempt to deny she was the cause of his erection, and he made no apology for it. It was heady to know this older, sophisticated man wanted her. Was she embarrassed? No, not really, though she wouldn't deny feeling flustered. "It's okay," she whispered shyly, eyes on his chest instead of his face, both because she was feeling insecure and because the tanned expanse of skin, dusted with black hair, was mesmerizing. Her fingers clenched as she imagined grabbing a handful to anchor herself as she leaned forward to kiss him. She could never be that bold, so she sat there, waiting to see what would happen next.

His hand cupped the back of her head again, grasping strands of her hair to gently pull up her head. "I can call a cab for you and have your car driven home, or I can let you walk out of here and drive yourself home, or..."

"Or?" she prompted, holding her breath.

"Or, you can stay the night with me, and I'll show you just how special your first time could be, Erin." Jared lowered his head, brushing his lips against hers in the lightest of kisses. "You have to decide what you want and take responsibility for the decision though."

Chapter Two

Erin craved another one of those kisses, but deeper and longer. Her hands itched to touch him, and she couldn't resist conjuring mental pictures of the two of them tangled on his massive bed. "I'd like to stay, Jared," she whispered, still feeling timid.

He gave her one more light kiss before pulling back again. "I'd like that too, but there's one more thing I need to know." At her nod, he said, "I want to make sure you want me, and this isn't some twisted way to get back at Chip. I will gladly spend all night making love to you, but only if it's me you really want."

Erin's eyes widened. "I hadn't even considered that, Mr.—Jared. I swear."

He looked deep into her eyes, looking satisfied. "Very well. Do you need to call your parents or anyone to let them know you won't be home?"

She shook her head. "I live with my older sister, and she knows I plan to be out all night." Though Megan was expecting her to be sleeping with Chip, not his father.

"Okay then." Finally, he guided her head closer, holding her tautly against him as his mouth settled over hers. Jared kissed her thoroughly, his tongue pushing between the seam of her lips to explore the interior.

Erin did her best to mimic his motions, before sensations overwhelmed her, and she couldn't consciously think about doing anything. Instead, she was a creature guided by impulse. In response to the stimuli flooding her body, she pushed her pussy against his cock, rubbing her wet folds against his hard flesh. The silk robe provided delicious friction, but seemed like an unbearable barrier to what her young body sought out instinctively.

Jared trailed his mouth from her lips and across her cheek, to her ear. As he nibbled and sucked on the lobe, she arched her neck, continuing to rub against him in a way that seemed to aggravate, rather than relieve, the ache inside her. "Oh, Jared, I need..." She broke off, not entirely sure what she needed. Understanding the semantics of sex was a different thing from experiencing them.

He lifted his head. "Shh, beautiful girl, I know what you need." He stood up abruptly, and she locked her legs around his waist as he carried her from the lounge to the bed across the room. The velvet cover under her back was decadent, as was the sight of Jared shedding his robe as he stood by the bed.

His body was hard and firm in all the right places. For a man who had to be at least forty, he didn't look it. Her eyes widened at the sight of his cock. It was certainly not a case of like father, like son. Chip was averagely endowed, where Jared had the complete package, and then some. It was daunting.

"Do you mind if I take off your shoes?" He grinned. "They're like deathtraps."

Erin giggled, releasing the heavy burden of hurt she'd still been holding onto since realizing how sleazy Chip was. "Go for it."

His long fingers were nimble with the buckles of the shoes. Even such a simple task as removing the platforms was rendered sensual by his slow strokes and gentle exploration. Erin gasped with surprise when he brought one of her feet to his mouth, sucking on the polished big toe in a way that dragged at the pit of her stomach and made her squeeze her thighs.

Jared grimaced slightly and released her toe. "You taste delicious, but the red nail polish has to go. Next time, please leave it off."

She thrilled at his confident assurance there would be a next time and nodded. "I might," she conceded mischievously. "If you'll make it worth my while." It was liberating, but still a bit scary, to be teasing Jared. Hell, the whole experience was a mixture of both.

His eyes sparkled. "That can be arranged." Taking a step back, he examined her for a moment, before his hands went to the tie on her dress.

Erin stiffened, feeling a flash of fear, but didn't protest. He hesitated for a second, as though giving her a chance to change her mind, before untying the bow and opening the dress.

That displayed a good part of her body right then, though her left breast remained covered. In seconds, he dealt with the interior tie and peeled back the other panel of fabric. She lay on the outfit, but it offered no shield. He stared at her, as though drinking her in, and she shivered with nerves.

As his gaze rested on her breasts, her nipples tightened, but she suddenly clapped her hands over them. He frowned and reached for her hands. Erin resisted his attempts to pull them away. "I'm too small," she whispered.

Jared shook his head. "Your breasts are perfect."

At his words, she stopped trying to cover them and let him move her hands. He got onto the bed with her, straddling her thighs, as he leaned forward. Jared pinned her wrists above her head, pushing her arms into the mattress, as he lowered his head. He kissed her for a long moment before moving his mouth to the side. Pausing near her ear, he said, "I think your breasts are gorgeous as they are, with those pointy little pink nipples, but there are ways to make them larger."

Her stomach dipped, and she was wounded. He couldn't really find her breasts perfect if he was suggesting surgery. "I would never get an operation."

Jared trailed his tongue across her chest and over her left breast, pausing to lave the nipple. "Honey, I didn't mean a surgical procedure. Someday, when you're pregnant, your breasts will get very large and firm." He sucked the nipple into his mouth. "You'll be full of milk for your baby." He looked up at her. "And your husband, if he's a lucky bastard."

"Oh." His words were deliciously naughty, making her think about something that had never occurred to her before. Breastfeeding was completely natural, the normal thing for mother and baby, but she'd never considered that some men might like such a thing too. "Do you like that?" she whispered.

"Mmm, I love this." He took more of her nipple into his mouth, his hands still holding hers against the bed. "It's plump and delicious," he added after sucking for another minute.

She was breathless. "Uh, okay, but I meant the milk thing."

Jared shrugged one shoulder. "I don't know. Chip's mother never breastfed, because it would ruin her breasts." He rolled his eyes. "I've never tried it, but I won't deny the sight of a pregnant woman, or a pair of lactating breasts, can turn me on under the right circumstances."

"Oh," she said softly. What would it be like to have his baby growing in her body, to have his mouth sucking her pregnant breasts? She moaned at the thought, finding it a lot hotter than she ever would have expected.

Jared let go of her hands to cup her breasts, pushing them together so the nipples almost touched. She gasped when he ran his tongue back and forth across both rapidly, occasionally flicking with the tip of his tongue or pausing to suck one. The sensation was indescribable, and her pussy was soaking wet in no time. She writhed under him, arching her hips, and lifting her buttocks off the bed as she sought relief. "Jared, please, I can't..."

He laughed, but lifted his head. "You can, honey."

Erin shook her head. "I'll die if you keep doing that."

Grasping her hips, he shifted his weight and moved her higher up the bed. "You'll die several times tonight, my sweet." He nudged her thighs apart, settling between them to put his face against her slit. He inhaled deeply before exhaling against her. His breath teased the sensitive flesh, and she whimpered, lifting her butt higher.

"Smooth," he said, sounding pleased and surprised.

"I waxed yesterday afternoon," she confided. Actually, one of the women at her sister's salon had helped her with the task, which had been painful, but clearly worth the effort judging by his appreciative noises.

"I do like a hairy pussy," he said, sounding not a bit self-conscious. "They're pretty and fun to look at, but a bald little kitty is so much tastier to eat." He licked one of her outer lips, trailing his tongue down the length, to her perineum, and then back up the other lip, seeming to take extra care not to touch her clit. "You should definitely keep your pussy smooth."

"Okay." She could endure the sting for a few minutes if it made her lover happy. And it sounded like Jared intended to be her lover, not just a one-night fling. Or was she misreading things? Was she trying to project more intent than was there? Hadn't she already done enough damage to herself by imagining emotions and feelings that didn't exist in her relationship with Chip? She couldn't afford to follow that path again. "Oh," she cried out, all thoughts leaving her mind as he continued licking her.

Jared ran the broad part of his tongue across her slit, the appendage squirming in to explore her. He swirled the tip around her clit a few times as she bucked mindlessly under him, before continuing his swipe downward, to dart his tongue in and out of her opening several times.

Then he did something so shocking that she grabbed a handful of his hair and screamed his name. His tongue went lower, sweeping down her perineum toward the dark hole waiting there. She cried out in protest when he breached the puckered ring. "Stop. You can't."

He paused, looking up briefly. "You don't like it?"

"Uh...I don't know." She hadn't really had a chance to experience the sensations. It had just been too outrageous, and she had reacted.

"In that case..." Jared trailed off, returning to the forbidden zone. His tongue teased and tickled her anus, briefly darting inside and around the hole. A feeling like electricity sparked through her lower half, and she pressed her ass tighter against his face.

Jared chuckled against her skin. "Thought so," he said with triumph, before returning to his taboo task. A moment later, he slipped a hand between her thighs, his finger and thumb seeking out her clit. He rolled the sensitive bud between his fingers as his tongue flicked over and into her back passage.

Erin twisted against him, her lower half completely off the bed, except for her heels. "Jared. Oh, it's so much. Too much." Slick heat drenched her folds seconds before her sheath tightened, and an orgasm rushed over her, making her entire body shake with the force of it.

"Good girl," he praised, as though she had done something amazing, when it was all him. She had just been at his mercy. Apparently, she was still at his mercy, because he shifted again, once more putting his mouth against her cunt, with his hands gripping her buttocks. He pulled her tightly against him, not allowing her room to squirm or escape as he began pussy-eating in earnest.

Powerless, Erin held onto the bedcovers with both hands, hating the way his hold constrained her movements, even as she recognized how much it heightened her pleasure. There was literally no escaping his hot, questing mouth. His only concession to her next release was a brief cessation of sucking and swirling, but then he wrung another and another climax from her, barely letting her finish the previous one before causing another.

Twenty minutes later, she lay on the bed, completely drained, though her pussy still pulsed with aftershocks. It had been an overwhelming experience, but she'd never been so sated—and he hadn't even put his cock inside her yet.

That reminded her that Jared must be feeling neglected. He was lying on his side next to her, as she remained sprawled on her back, legs gaping open. It would take way too much energy to close them. "I had no idea," she said in a slurred tone that made her sound like a strung-out junkie.

He smiled, looking pleased. "I hope you'll always remember this."

She nodded, already feeling a hint of sadness at the thought of this ending. "I'll never forget tonight." Mustering a bit of vigor, she reached out to touch his cock, tracing her fingers over the bulging veins and up to the tip, where pre-ejaculate flowed in steady drips. "He's big."

Jared grinned. "I'm a big man."

He was, at well over six feet, with his solid muscles and broad shoulders. Still, his cock seemed disproportionately large. "I'm not even sure he'd fit in my mouth." It was a half-teasing, half-serious declaration.

He made his cock jump by flexing his muscles. "We could find out."

Erin smiled, finding it easier to move as the languid pleasure slowly faded from her body. "Yes, we could." She slithered down the bed a bit, turning on her side to face his cock. The head nudged against her lips, and she parted them to take a small taste of his pre-cum. He was salty, but with an underlying hint of sweetness. It wasn't at all unpleasant. Looking up his body, she met his gaze, pleased to see how his gray eyes looked like dark pools of melted platinum. "I've never done this before, Jared."

"Just do what feels right."

Closing her eyes, Erin put her mouth around him, grimacing a bit at the girth. He really was large enough that she doubted her ability to engulf him completely. Patience and lots of saliva proved to be the solution, and he was soon in her mouth to the point where his head rested at the back of her tongue.

Experimentally, she twirled her tongue around the shaft, paying attention to the way he groaned when the broad part of her tongue pressed against the underside of his cock. She focused on that area, applying pressure with her tongue that she alternated with licks. Erin also tried sucking him, but it was awkward with his size.

"Suck in your cheeks," he said, placing his hand at the back of her head. When she complied, he began to thrust gently in and out of her mouth, slowly pushing the limits of how deeply she could take him. "Try to relax your throat so I can go in deeper, baby."

Erin concentrated on relaxing, doing her best not to panic at the choking sensation as he sank deeper inside her mouth. After a moment, the sensation of not being able to breathe passed, and while it wasn't exactly comfortable, she could hold him inside her throat. Cautiously, she returned to sucking him as he rocked in and out of her, fucking her face with slow strokes.

His fluid was increasing, coating her tongue and dripping down her throat. Putting a hand on his ass to steady herself, she could feel the muscles twitching underneath her skin and figured he must be getting close to coming.

Abruptly, Jared pulled out of her mouth and shifted to straddle her. The head of his cock probed at her entrance as he repositioned her. "I want to be inside you so badly, Erin."

She smiled, heart racing with excitement that she would soon lose her virginity, and to a man she had never expected. "I want that too."

He looked annoyed, but she soon realized not with her. "I don't have any condoms here. I wasn't expecting anything like this, and I haven't been seeing anyone recently." Looking hopeful, he said, "Did you bring some for your planned night with Chip?"

Erin frowned. "No. He has a whole drawer full, literally."

Jared pushed in an inch or so, staying in her untried passage for a moment before withdrawing. "I suppose I could ask Mr. Edwin to bring some from my son's room." Again, he thrust into her, going a little deeper, to the barrier of her hymen, where he froze. "That would require tearing myself away from your pretty pussy for a few minutes."

"Plus, it could be awkward." She couldn't stifle a giggle as she imagined Chip's outrage at his dad bumming condoms so he could fuck his ex-girlfriend. A dark, twisted part of her liked that scenario.

Easing out, he pushed back in again slowly, this time to her hymen and a bit beyond. The stretched, burning sensation made her shift uncomfortably, and he put his hand between them to find her clit. "Still, it's the only alternative."

As his fingers fondled her clit, she arched against him, bringing his cock a bit deeper inside her. "Maybe you could pull out at the end?"

He groaned, letting his body in a bit deeper as his fingers continued working her slick button. "That's a good idea."

"Definitely," she said, thrusting against him as his cock breached her hymen, ripping through the delicate barrier as gently as he could. It elicited a startled cry from her, but his fingers on her clit soon soothed the pain.

"God, you're tight, Erin." He sank deeper, taking her an inch at a time. "I've never had such a tight pussy around me."

"I hope that's a good thing." She moaned as he pinched her clit and slipped in deeper.

"It's amazing, but I'm afraid I might not pull out in time." Jared bottomed out inside her, his balls pressing against her labia, and his cock stretching her pussy to the point where she didn't know if she wanted to scream from pleasure, pain, or both.

"Oh, that could be a problem." It was hard to focus on any problems with a man's huge cock buried completely inside her. The head rested against her cervix.

"Yes." He seemed to be straining to hold back his release as he withdrew a couple of inches before slowing thrusting into her again. "What was your last period?"

That was an embarrassingly intimate topic, though she knew it was ridiculous to feel shy about it when they were having sex. "About two weeks ago."

He groaned. "Two weeks from the beginning or the end?"

It took a moment to focus as he continued stroking her clit and thrusting into her, alternating shallow and deep strokes. "Um, beginning."

Jared cursed. "Okay, I have to pull out now. It's too risky." He said the words, but he didn't move. His face was red with exertion, and he seemed to be struggling with the decision.

"Oh, don't leave." She tightened her thighs around his waist, clamping him against her. The thought of him pulling out of her body before taking her over the precipice again was unbearable.

"I don't want to, honey, but you could get pregnant." He cursed again. "It's way too likely, since you're young and no doubt fertile." He said the last part with a groan of pain. "I'm sure your womb is ready, and there's an egg just waiting for a sperm to come along." A growl of pleasure accompanied his next thrust into her, and he let the full length rest inside her. "If I keep going, you'll swell up with my baby inside you. Is that what you want?" The husky exhilaration tingeing his tone suggested he liked the idea a lot.

"Yes," she shouted, honestly convinced it was the best idea ever. If the alternative was this bond ending prematurely, of having him pull away from her and facing the possibility of never feeling this way again, she'd agree to have ten babies with him, all at once. "Fill me with your cum, Jared. I don't care what happens tomorrow. I need you right now."

He groaned, his hand leaving her clit to slide under her ass. "I'll take care of you," he promised with clear sincerity. "Whatever happens." As he thrust in and out of her, he angled her hips a bit, so his cock hit a spot deep inside her that made her cry out and flex around him. "You're mine now, Erin."

"Yours," she consented, matching his thrusts as the fire burned low in her belly, spreading outward with such strength that her entire body shuddered and shook. "Make me yours, Jared."

His cock convulsed inside her as her passage clamped around him, wringing every drop of his precious cum from his dick. Her orgasm crashed over her, and tears streamed from her eyes. She sobbed his name as she came, and Jared gave a hoarse shout as he sank deeply inside her, spilling the last bit of his essence against her cervix, where it would have easy passage to her possibly waiting egg.

Eventually, the euphoria passed enough for them to separate a bit, roll onto their sides, and cuddle on the velvet comforter. Erin rubbed her cheek against his chest, trying to remove the moisture there.

"I meant it," he said quietly.

She looked up, chin propped on his sternum. "What?"

"I meant that I'll take care of you. If you want the morning-after pill, I'll get it for you. If you want to see what happens, I'm okay with that too. If you get pregnant, I'll provide for you however you want me to."

Her eyes stung with tears. "Dammit, I've done nothing but cry today," she said with a soggy smile. "These are good tears," she hastened to assure him. "You're wonderful, Jared. I feel so safe and protected."

"I feel amazing," he said softly, burying his hands in her hair to caress the now-frizzy curls. "I've wanted you for so long."

Her eyes widened. "What?"

Jared looked uncomfortable. "It's not easy to want to have your son's girlfriend, to think about her, fantasize about her." He cupped one of her breasts, lightly rubbing the nipple. "I've imagined you like this a hundred times in the last couple of months, since the first night Chip brought you home to meet me."

"Oh." That was unexpected, and maybe a tad alarming. How could such a hot, confident man like him lust after her? She was only a few months into her first semester of college and had nothing to offer him. She voiced the thought aloud. "You can't want me, Jared. I'm nothing. I have nothing. I don't even have parents. They're both losers. If my older sister wasn't so decent, I'd still be living in foster care."

He shrugged. "I don't give a damn about any of that." His hand crept lower, to cover her stomach. "Besides, you can give me something I want very much, and that's a family. I've always wanted more children, and someday, if you're ready, I'd like you to be their mother. I want you."

Her head whirled, and she blinked, certain she was dreaming. "You mean, like long-term want me?" At his nod, she blinked again. "Wow." How did she respond to that? "Well, that's…"

"Overwhelming and too much pressure," he said decisively. "I'm not going to force you into anything. I wouldn't even try to compel you to have my baby if you get pregnant tonight. That's your decision."

Erin shook her head. "Termination is not a decision I would ever make. I support a woman's right to decide for herself, but I already know I couldn't have an abortion, except maybe under some very limited circumstances."

He seemed pleased. "That still leaves you the option of emergency contraceptive. Shall I send Mr. Edwin to the drugstore?"

Erin giggled, trying to imagine the stuffy, starched butler buying Plan B. "No, that's an indignity from which he might never recover."

"Well, you have ninety-six hours to take it, if you decide to."

Snuggling closer, she licked his nipple before responding. "I don't think I will. I kind of feel like this was all fate or something. Like tonight was supposed to happen, so whatever happens was meant to as well." She frowned. "Is that hopelessly ridiculous?"

He shook his head. "It's beautiful."

Scooting closer, Erin put her arm around him. "So, will you marry me if I'm pregnant?" It was a bold question, but she was only partially teasing. She yearned to know just how serious he was, and how long-term he envisioned.

"Honey, I'd marry you if you weren't pregnant," he said with utter conviction. "I'd fly you to Vegas tonight and elope if you'd let me." Jared put up a hand. "But I'm not suggesting that. This is all new, and you deserve time to adjust, to figure out if this is what you want."

"Plus, I have to tell my sister." She drew her bottom lip between her teeth. Megan might not be thrilled to find out she was contemplating a relationship with a man old enough to be her father. Flexing her hand, she caressed his abs. Not that he looked or felt like a father.

"So, we wait and see what happens?"

She nodded. "I think I know what might happen next." Wrapping her hand around his semi-flaccid cock, she stroked him to hardness again.

"I think you might be a fortune teller," said Jared with a laugh, drawing her against him for a repeat performance.

Epilogue

Eighteen months later, Erin married Jared with their nine-month-old daughter near them, in Aunt Megan's arms. It hadn't been a shock to find herself pregnant after that night, especially since they'd indulged in several more careless nights that week, before making an effort to get birth control. Being pregnant hadn't meant she was ready for such a serious step as marriage, and they had spent a lot of time getting to know each other and deciding their futures belonged together.

As she danced in her husband's arms, with Zoe cuddled between them, she looked around. Chip was over at the bar, sloppy drunk and with his arm around some girl, who seemed to have borrowed a dress that was two sizes too small. She felt a well of pity for the boy who was now her stepson, but that was it. Chip didn't approve of their marriage, but she couldn't do anything to change that. All she could do was ensure her husband still offered support and communicated with Chip, while hoping he sorted everything out before fucking up his life permanently.

Zoe squealed, earning both her parents' attention. "I think she's wet," said Jared.

Her breasts were aching, and she shook her head. "No, I think she needs to nurse." It was past time, going by Zoe's usual pattern. "We'll just slip away to the dressing room for a few minutes."

He nodded, his eyes on her milk-heavy breasts, displayed to full advantage by the cut of the dress. "Save some for me," he said with a wink.

"You're depraved," she said with an indulgent chuckle, unwilling to admit just how erotic she found it when he sucked on her milk-laden breasts. It was completely different from when Zoe did it, of course. With her baby, it was a warmly maternal thing. With Jared, it transformed into something hot, naughty, and mutually satisfying.

His eyes grew serious, and he drew her forward for a deep kiss. "I love you, Mrs. Maxwell."

Erin drew back a bit, finding it difficult to tear herself from her husband's embrace, even though milk was starting to trickle into the pads protecting her wedding dress. "I love you too, Mr. Maxwell." Later that night, she would find several ways to remind him just how much.

. . ⚬ . .

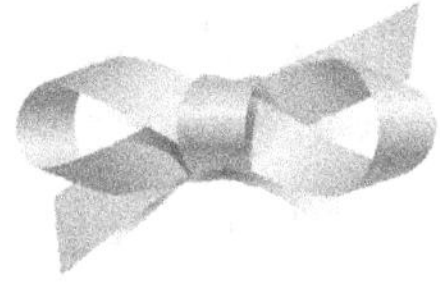

Bonus Excerpt from Kristianna

IF YOU ENJOYED "ERIN'S Unexpected Lover," please continue reading for an excerpt of "Snowbound," also by Kristianna Sawyer.

Planning to surprise her father, Beth Wyndam arrives at Reed Nixon's Alaskan guide facility a day earlier than the rest of her party. Terrible weather snows her in with the surly older man, but she finds herself drawn to him despite his grumpiness. Reed wants her too, but the fifteen years separating them, along with the differences in their backgrounds, are obstacles he can't bring himself to ignore. With a little luck, a lot of snow, and a power outage, Beth gets Reed in her bed. It's everything she had hoped, but the real challenge is not falling in love with a man who warned from the start there was no future for them—especially when she realizes there will be a permanent reminder of their affair.

Reed Nixon was in a foul mood, and he had no trouble admitting it. His coffeepot had broken that morning, and it was a damned pain in the ass to replace, living way up north. He'd have to special order it, have it shipped to Fairbanks, and then delivered via a charter company to Endline. After that, he'd have to drive two hundred miles down Dalton Highway in his rugged SUV, and that was a trip he hadn't planned on for at least another three months, until after the last of the worst weather passed for the season.

On top of that, he'd discovered a hole in his favorite snow boots, and one of the strings on his crossbow—that had cost almost as much as the SUV—was fraying, necessitating changing, which could be a time-consuming process, even for someone who knew a crossbow inside and out.

So, the last thing he felt like was greeting his arriving clients early. The Wyndam party wasn't scheduled to arrive until tomorrow. He'd been toying with the idea of contacting the charter service to see if his pal

Mike was flying in the guests. If so, he'd planned to ask Mike to bring him any kind of coffee machine, as long as it dispensed the thick, dark, and hot drink he needed to feel semi-human of a morning.

Knowing that wasn't happening was part of the reason he was so surly as he shrugged on his coat and boots, stomping through the snow to the airfield he'd had put in a few years ago, when he'd launched his guide business. He'd be the first to acknowledge that he was generally surly anyway, as a rule.

When the small plane landed, he threw up his hands, waiting until the door opened, and the stairs descended. "I wasn't expecting you until tomorrow, Wyndam," he started to snarl. His mouth snapped shut for just a minute as a petite figure in a bulky white parka and cumbersome white snow boots stepped down the stairs carefully.

As she drew nearer, he demanded, "Who the hell are you? Wyndam told me it'd be just him and his camera crew. He didn't say nothin' about his girlfriend comin' along." She flinched at the rough tone, and he felt a spark of regret when he noticed how young she was. That fled when she opened her mouth.

"I'm his daughter, not his girlfriend, and who the hell are you?" She asked the question in exactly the same tone he had. "Daddy said the tour guide would meet me, but that can't be you."

Her dismissive look rose his hackles—and brought back some of his old insecurities from growing up dirt-poor and the son of the town drunk. "Why can't that be me, sweetheart?" He practically snarled the question at her.

If she was at all intimidated, it didn't show. "Someone getting paid to take care of a group wouldn't be so unprofessional."

He opened his mouth, but then shut it for a moment, deciding she had a point. "I'm sorry," he said, still gruffly. "I wasn't expecting nobody 'til tomorrow."

She nodded. "I guess you needed that extra twenty-four hours to find your manners, huh?"

Just like that, the little hellion set his teeth back on-edge. In an attempt to control his irritation, he walked to the pilot, who wasn't Mike. He thought this one was Vic, who mainly flew charters out of Fairbanks. "Vic?" At the man's nod, he held out his hand, more to show the irritating kitten beside him that he had some manners than because he actually felt compelled to make a friendly greeting. "How're you doin'?" After a quick exchange of pleasantries, he asked, "Where's the rest of 'em?"

Vic shrugged. "Don't know. Got a call asking us to fly in Ms. Wyndam today, and still plan on bringing the rest tomorrow."

With a small sigh, he turned back to face the young woman. "Ms. Wyndam, where is the rest of your party?"

She gave him a sweet smile, but her green eyes still crackled with banked anger. "They're still in Endline and planning to come tomorrow, as scheduled. I happened to arrive early, so Daddy arranged for the charter company to pick me up in Fairbanks and deliver me here."

He nodded just once. "Well, where's your gear?" He expected to be hauling suitcases into the guest quarters for the next hour, so it was a bit of a surprise to have Vic hand him just one large suitcase. "You just staying overnight?" he joked, as he lifted the suitcase, bade Vic goodbye, and led the girl—young woman—toward the guest quarters.

She frowned. "No, I'm here for a couple of weeks. Why?"

He lifted the bag a bit higher. "Most women I've seen come here," and he could count the number on one hand, "Bring a mountain of luggage."

"Oh. Daddy mentioned he was packing light, but bringing lots of warm things." Her smile seemed genuine. "I have to warn you that my dad's idea of light packing is a lot different than mine."

He waved a hand. "A girl who listens to her father. That's unusual in your generation."

She rolled her eyes. "My generation? What are you, ten minutes older than me?"

A genuine laugh burst from him. "Sweetheart, I'm thirty-three."

As he opened the door that allowed the guests their own private entrance and exit, he moved aside to let her pass. She paused right in front of him, leaning against the doorway for a moment in her puffy white parka. "Well, sweetheart, I'm eighteen. That's hardly another generation."

She slipped on past him, turning back to look over her shoulder as she added, "And I only listen to my father when I feel like it."

Feeling slightly bemused, he followed her into his house, quickly overtaking her shorter stride, to give her the brief tour. "This is the guests' quarters. There are two rooms. A small private room, and a larger room with six bunks." He gestured to a door nearby. "You go through there for the commode." Farther down the wood-paneled hall, he pointed to another door. "That leads to the kitchen. It's shared space with my residence, but you're welcome to help yourself to anything. I hope your daddy told you to bring any special thing you wanted along. I keep the basics, and then some, but I don't offer no fancy stuff."

"Darn," she said with a small hint of mocking. "I guess I should have packed champagne and caviar instead of my pants."

The idea of this young woman running around in no pants caused a sudden hitch in his breathing. He didn't reply to the sarcasm as he led her to the small private room with its double bed. "You'll have to make do with this. I laid out toiletries for a man, expecting Mr. Wyndam to stay in this room. He didn't say nothin' about a girl," he reminded.

"Yeah, I know. Daddy isn't one for bragging about his children." She said it offhandedly, as though it was no big deal, but he thought there was a hint of hurt underneath. Or maybe he was just projecting his own rotten childhood onto her.

He set her bag down on the trunk at the foot of the bed, near the rustic log footboard he'd made himself. "I'll leave you to unpack, Ms. Wyndam. I fix dinner around six, unless you prefer to look after yourself." He wanted to scoff at the thought. It seemed clear to him that the little princess in front of him wasn't used to doing much for herself. Apparently, making documentaries was a lot more lucrative than he'd ever imagined, judging from her appearance and demeanor. He knew for a fact the coat she wore cost several thousand dollars. He had one from the same designer, but it was their Outlet line, and he'd had to save three years to afford it. Of course, he'd never need another one. Point was, quality costs, and she'd clearly paid a lot. Well, her Daddy's Amex had, he thought, with a grimace of distaste.

She smiled. "Thank you, Mr....?"

"Reed."

"Mr. Reed."

He shook his head, sending shaggy brown strands falling into his eyes. "Nah, just Reed. Reed Nixon."

She chose that moment to push back the hood of her parka and take off the soft-looking light-pink hat underneath. A mass of silvery-blonde hair fell free, and even the confining ponytail couldn't keep all the determined strands tamed. He had the insane urge to bury his hand in the tresses and tug her closer. Thankfully, it was a notion that passed quickly, and he took a step back to make sure he didn't do anything asinine.

"Well, thanks, just Reed. I'm Beth." She stripped off her gloves before tackling the zipper. "Goodness, my fingers are frozen," she said. Struggling with the coat, she looked disconcertingly like a little girl for a moment.

Reed stepped quickly to the door. "I'll get a fire started in the common area. Just through that door, same as the kitchen." Without awaiting a response, he ducked out of the room and back into his own quarters. It took every ounce of self-control not to bolt the door that separated his house from the guestrooms, as though he could lock out his unexpected reaction by keeping the door between them barred.

"You're losin' it, man," he said softly to himself, as he went to build up the fire that was little more than a smoldering crackle at the moment.

Beth didn't believe in love at first sight. That was nonsense you read about in romance books, or saw in movies. She certainly hadn't fallen for Reed Nixon on sight. He'd been surly and short-tempered, and not at all charming or warm. Nope, definitely not on sight. As she brushed out her hair and smoothed down her sweater, nerves made her stomach jump, and she tried to decide at what point she'd fallen in lust—not love—with the grouchy guide.

Her lips twitched as she remembered the pointed way he'd shaken the pilot's hand. The only thing missing had been him sticking his tongue out at her and saying, "Neener, neener, neener." Yeah, that was about the time she'd realized there was more to him than just a grump.

His voice was deep and rough, with a rich southern twang that seemed a little out of place in the Far North region. She liked it though, and it didn't take too much imagination to have him whispering all sorts of naughty things in her head as she got ready to join him for dinner.

Leaning forward to touch up her lip-gloss, she met her own eyes in the mirror and grinned. He'd be the type to speak plainly, and probably earthily, rather than vaguely or whimsically. She had a feeling Reed was the kind of man who would tell a woman he wanted to fuck her, instead of asking to make love to her.

Considering the boys she knew—and none of them could be counted as men when compared to Reed—were all the romance and flowers type, she thought it would be refreshing to have a real man telling her bluntly what he wanted her to do. Or do to her, she imagined with a small shiver.

Of course, she had to get him to notice her as more than a paying client's daughter first. It was obvious he considered her a little girl, and a real man had no interest in little girls.

A quick glance at the gold watch on her wrist revealed it was five until six, so she slipped out of the room and down the hall. Pausing at the door, she took one more deep breath for courage before opening it to enter the common area.

She let her gaze dance around the interior, finding it was more paneled wood, rustic timber supports, and some type of white stone accents. There was a large fur on the floor near the fireplace, and she frowned at it. She knew Reed ran a guide business, and that included taking clients out to hunt, but she didn't approve. Thankfully, her daddy wasn't one of those idiot outdoorsmen, preferring to do his shooting with a camera instead of a gun. He was here to make a documentary on the wildlife of the Far North.

The small great room led right into the kitchen, which held a dining table big enough for eight. She paused to admire the raw log legs before running a hand over the smooth wood. "This is pretty. Where'd you get it?"

He looked up from the stove for the first time since she entered the room, though she was positive he'd seen her the moment she opened the door from the guest quarters.

"I made it myself. Pretty much have to if you want something out here."

So, he had skilled hands. That thought made her tingle between the thighs, and she pressed them together discreetly. "Can I help with anything?"

He looked surprised by the offer, along with more than a tad disbelieving. "Nah, I got it. Just some stew and cornbread."

She nodded, taking a seat beside the chair at the head of the table, which she correctly assumed would be his. He didn't seem to like her proximity, and she had a moment of doubt. Could she really get this man to see her as a woman, not just an inconvenient adolescent?

He set a big bowl of stew down, along with a basket of cornbread. She was a little surprised to find he'd wrapped the bread in a red-checked cloth. He was so male, so raw and rough, that she wouldn't have been surprised if he'd served the stew in the pot and the cornbread still in the pan.

She helped herself to some of both and spooned up a bite of the stew. "Wow, this is good. What brand is it?"

He blinked. "Brand?"

Beth arched a brow. "You know, like what company put it in the can?"

Reed made a scoffing sound. "Ain't no can, girl. I made it. Like I said, you want something in this environment, you gotta know how to make it." He gave her an unreadable look. "Lot of folks like comin' here for trips and such, but they ain't got what you need to survive out here."

She bristled at the implication she wasn't tough or able to make do. Just because she never had didn't mean she couldn't. Still, arguing with him seemed counterproductive to trying to seduce him, so she bit her tongue. Her seduction plans were looking less likely with every passing minute though. Her dad and the film crew would be joining them tomorrow, and she doubted there'd be any opportunities after that.

"Well, it's delicious. What's in it?"

If he found the question as stupid as it was, he was nice enough not to be too obvious. "Potatoes, carrots, onions, garlic, gravy, and caribou."

She frowned, putting down her spoon. "Caribou?"

He nodded. "You got a problem with that? You seemed to be enjoyin' it a moment ago."

Beth grimaced. "I don't approve of hunting when there's food in the grocery store."

Reed laughed, and it was more than a bit mocking. "Where'd you think that food comes from, girl? The cow fairy?"

She frowned. "I'm not a girl, and I know where it comes from. Those animals are raised in captivity. They wouldn't know how to survive if you set them free, unlike the wildlife."

He snorted. "So you're doing a favor by killing them?" He didn't wait for a reply. "Have you ever seen a concentrated animal feeding operation, Beth?" When she shook her head, he said, "I have. I worked one summer at a pig company. It was brutal. Those animals are mistreated from the moment they're born until they're finally put outta their misery—and half the time, that's done half-assed too, so they suffer 'til the very end." He took a big bite of his stew, as though for emphasis. "I'd rather know the animal I'm eating lived the life it was supposed to and was killed humanely. I don't let them suffer."

She hated to concede, but he had a point, and a way of making her look at it that she hadn't considered before. "Okay, but what about the sport hunters you guide?"

He lifted a shoulder. "Some of them take the meat, and some don't, but I don't let none of it go to waste. If the hunters only want their trophies, they take whatever token they think is important, and I keep the rest. Sometimes I eat it, and sometimes it goes to folks that need it more. I usually end up dropping off a couple hundred pounds of meat in Endline for the town folks when I go twice a year to replenish supplies."

"Oh." She didn't look up at him again as she took another tentative bite of the meat. "What about if you have a hunter who just injures the animal?"

He sighed. "That's happened a few times. Usually, it's some pansy-assed stockbroker, or somethin', who couldn't keep up with me for miles, so I end up tracking the animal and finishing it off. If it's not too bad, I try to save it and let it go back to its life. And I never accept those incompetent assholes as clients again."

"Oh," she said again, nodding. "That's very decent of you."

He rolled his eyes, as though she had insulted him instead of complimented him. "Thanks, girl."

"I'm not a girl," she said again, more firmly.

With an ambiguous look, he turned his attention back to his bowl. "I know that," he mumbled, saying nothing else throughout the meal.

Of course she wasn't a girl. Stripped of that parka and wearing those tight jeans—were they called skinny jeans?—and a snug sweater in that same sort of some material as her hat, there was no mistaking her for a girl. She had nicely rounded breasts, long legs for her frame that seemed built to wrap around a man's waist, and curvy hips that could take the pressure of a man's hands holding them while he pounded into her.

Fuck, she was definitely not a girl. He stirred the fire with the poker as he listened to her sing softly while she put away the dishes she had insisted on washing. He'd half-expected to have to redo them himself, but after watching her for a couple of minutes, he'd realized she could handle the task. It might be the first time she'd ever done them, but washing dishes wasn't exactly brain surgery.

Not that he'd count her out of that profession, or any other. She was obviously well educated and came from money. Smart and sassy, only a fool would underestimate her prospects.

Only a goddamn fool would be imagining what it might be like to taste the honeyed skin of her neck, or cup her ass in his hands, knowing the kind of man he was. He'd left most of his past behind when he'd come to Alaska eight years ago, but he was smart enough to know a woman like that was out of his league. Never mind the fifteen years separating them. His past and her future would never mesh, so fantasizing about touching that luscious woman was plain foolishness.

When her daddy and crew arrived tomorrow, he'd have to be damned sure he hid any hint of attraction he felt. The Wyndam group was paying enough for him to be able to take a season off and have some personal space again. After a few months of people, he always got fed up and had to have a breather. He couldn't risk alienating such clients, and hitting on the teenage daughter, even if she was technically legal, was a surefire way to do so.

What was wrong with him anyway, that he was feeling lustful for a teenager? Dammit, he should have stopped by the whorehouse the last time he was in Endline. In a region where men were far more common than women, it was about the only sure thing a man could find in these parts. Most women were already partnered up with someone, and since he wasn't the partnering-up type, whores were a viable option. The last couple of trips though, he'd passed on by the nondescript house on the edge of the city, finding the idea of meaningless sex that he paid for was no more satisfying or appealing than his own hand.

Now, he wished he'd dipped his dick in all six of the whores working there, with the appropriate raingear, of course. Apparently, his body was feeling the itch for feminine companionship, and if he'd scratched it three months ago, he wouldn't be stifling back a groan at the sight of that sweetly rounded ass in those tight jeans as she bent over to put the stewpot into the drawer under the oven.

She joined him all too quickly, and he was equal parts disappointed and relieved when she sat down on the same couch as him, instead of heading on to her room. At least she left a cushion between them. Damn, didn't the girl have any common sense? She was alone with a man she didn't know, and he could take advantage of her without her consent, if he was a different sort. Hell, didn't her daddy have any common sense? Who sent their teenage daughter to a strange man's home alone? Without thought, he voiced his opinion. "What kind of stupid is your father that he just lets you travel alone and sends you wherever without a proper escort?"

She cocked her head, looking both amused and angry. "He didn't let me travel anywhere. I'm an adult, and I booked my ticket. I'd planned to stay in Fairbanks and just meet up with him for a few days in Edgeline."

"Endline," he interrupted.

She waved a hand. "Yeah, whatever. Except I didn't realize the distance, or the difficulty with traveling. I thought I'd surprise him, but it ended up being an inconvenience." Beth shrugged. "Same as always, I guess."

"Still, his solution was to send his little girl on ahead to stay alone with a strange man?" He shook his head. "Ain't no way in hell my daughter would do such a foolish thing. I could be all kinds of pervert, girl."

She did grin then. "Really? What kinds are you?"

That wasn't the response he'd expected, and he was disconcerted to have his cheeks warming. "That's not the point. I'm just surprised by how lax y'all are with safety."

Beth's lips twitched. "I guess Daddy figured you'd be a professional, since you have a bazillion good references from previous guests." She shrugged. "Or maybe he didn't think at all. I'm not high on his list of priorities."

His frown deepened. "Then he needs to reorder his priorities." At her careless shrug, his irritation softened, and he warred with the urge to pick up her hand and offer comfort. Only the knowledge that innocent comfort could lead to carnal actions kept his hand firmly on his own leg. "What about you? Don't you have more regard for your safety?"

"I can take care of myself."

She spoke with such conviction that he couldn't help scoffing, though it probably insulted her. "Look, girl—"

"Beth," she put in.

"Beth," he repeated with gritted teeth. "You couldn't take on a wet kitten and win."

She cocked a brow. "Challenge accepted."

"Huh?" He frowned. "I don't actually have a wet kitten, you know," he said drily after a moment.

Beth's obstinate expression hardened further. "Get up."

"What?"

She got to her feet, moving lightly. "Come on. Get off your ass and come at me, Mr. All Kinds of Perv."

Feeling amused, and a tad indulgent, he stood up. He wasn't going to hurt her none, but a little lesson wouldn't be a bad idea. Ms. Wyndam needed to know she wasn't as tough as she thought, before she was actually in a situation that led her to act with foolish overconfidence. "All right, little girl. I'm gonna school you."

She didn't reply, just poising on the balls of her feet as she waited for him to make a move. Something about her stance annoyed him, and he found himself taking it more seriously than he'd intended. His first plan had been a direct assault, but he found himself drawing on the training he'd learned in the Army. He came at her to the right, before switching to the left at the last minute.

He'd expected to end up with her struggling in his arms, so the knee she rammed into his stomach was a shock. Reed let out a harsh breath and dropped to his knees from a combination of pain and surprise. In two seconds, that little hellcat kicked his shoulder, sending him reeling backward. She landed on his chest with enough force to make him exhale loudly, and her fingers hesitated within millimeters of his eyes. "Now, this is the point where I'd blind you, or rip your balls off..." She patted his thigh just an inch below his package. "If you were really trying to hurt me."

With a sunny smile, she bounded off him, offering him a hand up that he disdained. She shrugged and returned to the couch. "Poor loser."

He wasn't seriously injured, aside from his pride, and he was on his feet quickly, glaring down at her as he rubbed the sore spot on his shoulder. "How'd you learn all that?"

She smiled breezily. "I was into those martial arts movies for a while, so my mom got me private lessons. I know a couple of formal types of martial arts, but my instructor also taught me some dirty tricks."

"I'll say." He was reluctantly impressed as he sat down in his former spot.

"So, *kitten*," she asked sweetly, "Do you think I can take care of myself?"

"I sure hope so. After that kung fu shit, I'm relying on you to take care of me too, if bad guys come."

"No bad guys here," she said with a grin.

With more seriousness than he'd intended, he said, "Don't be too sure, Beth."

She regarded him for a moment, as though peering deep into his soul. "No bad guys here," she said again, and then lightened the mood by patting his thigh. "But I'll protect you if they show up."

He laughed with her, all the while conscious of her hand on his leg, and the way her breasts strained against the soft sweater as she leaned across the gap separating them to be able to touch him. His amusement fled as he contemplated grabbing a handful of the hair she'd brushed into a shining curtain of silvery blonde and bridging the distance. She couldn't weigh more than a hundred pounds, and he didn't think she'd resist if he lifted her to sit on his lap. It had been a while since a woman had desired him for any reason besides being paid to, but he was pretty sure he remembered that smoky look that came to her eyes, or the way an aroused woman licked her pouty lips.

If Beth wanted him, he was in big trouble. Her father couldn't arrive soon enough to save him from making a mistake that he seemed helpless to stop. Getting through the evening without touching her was an exercise in will power, and he was relieved when she started yawning around nine and made her way to bed. Thank goodness the rest of the group was coming tomorrow. His tenuous self-control needed reinforcements.

[Learn more](http://kittunstall.com/kit-tunstall-writing-as/kristianna-sawyer/)[1]

---

1. http://kittunstall.com/kit-tunstall-writing-as/kristianna-sawyer/

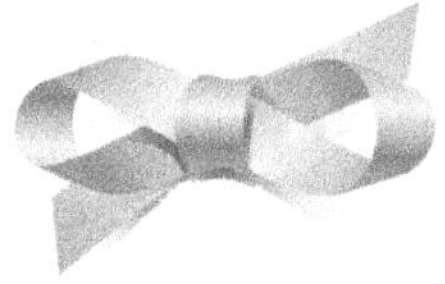

Sweet Candy

Another streak of lightning flashed across the sky when Gib opened the door. Rain still fell in torrents, having soaked his guest to the skin. "Candy?"

The girl flashed one of her bright smiles. "Hello, Mr. Olsen."

He opened the door, doing his best to keep his gaze from straying to her fantastic breasts, with the quarter-size nipples prominently displayed by her thin sundress. "Come in. I didn't know you were home from college yet."

Candy slipped inside, pushing soaking blonde strands of hair off her rounded face. "I got in late last night. Becca told me to come over tonight."

He smiled, imaging how excited his daughter would be to see her best friend. They'd gone to separate colleges for their freshman year—Candy off to an Ivy League school on the East coast, and Becca to the local community college, which was more in line with their budget. "She isn't home right now, Candy. She texted me a while ago that her boss is keeping her late. I guess the weather kept the night cashier from getting to the store."

Candy's expression revealed her disappointment. "Oh. Can you tell her I stopped by?"

Suddenly anxious to keep her from leaving, he put a hand on her arm. "Why don't you wait? It can't be that much longer."

It was adorable the way she nibbled on her lower lip while considering. Gib tried to quash the thought of how it would feel to run his tongue over her full lips.

After a brief hesitation, she nodded, and he closed the door behind her as she stepped fully into the living room. When she shivered, he turned toward the hallway. "Let me get you a towel. I'm sure Becca wouldn't mind if you borrowed some of her clothes."

Candy trailed behind him, laughing softly. "Thanks, Mr. Olsen, but I don't think I could squeeze into anything Becca wears. Too fat," she said matter-of-factly.

He frowned. "You aren't fat." Gib handed her a towel. Luscious was one way to describe her full curves. Divine was another adjective he could pull out of his stash to label those huge tits. She'd be the kind of woman that was soft and sweet to fuck, with her curves cushioning a man's harder planes. His cheeks heated with the beginnings of a flush, and he added, rather lamely, "You're healthy."

She smiled, seeming at-ease, though her expression betrayed her discomfort. "Thanks for the effort, Mr. Olsen, but you're a dad. You have to say that."

"I'm not *your* dad, Candy." He cleared his throat, discomfited by the husky note in his tone. "Let me see what I can find for you."

He moved past her as she slipped into the bathroom, praying his daughter's friend couldn't see the hard-on pressing against the seam of his zipper with a pressure guaranteed to leave marks. Gib went into his stepson's room. Danny was out doing who knew what tonight, but he didn't think the kid would begrudge Candy a shirt, so he helped himself to one without bothering trying to track him down via cell phone to ask.

He knocked on the door and passed the shirt through when she extended her hand. Gib's mind insisted on conjuring images of the buxom young lady in Danny's shirt. He took refuge in the kitchen, to order a pizza, and discovered his imagination couldn't compare to the real thing when she came in a few minutes later. The worn cotton clung to her curves, caressing her bust as thoroughly as he longed to. The light gray color obscured her areolas, but a dusky pink still showed through.

In an attempt to distract himself, he fumbled for the cordless phone, sending it spinning across the counter and onto the floor. Gib couldn't bite back a stifled groan when she knelt to pick it up, displaying her rounded bottom and pink panties—rendered slightly translucent from the rainwater that had soaked her clothes. The sight of her puffy pussy lips made his cock jerk. Muttering a hasty excuse, and shoving the stack of coupons across the counter toward the object of his lust, he rushed from the kitchen.

. . ❧ . .

MR. OLSEN'S SUDDEN departure surprised Candy, until she caught a glimpse of his raging erection as he hurried past her. Eyes wide, she made an effort to look at the pizza coupons, but couldn't get her mind off the thought that her best friend's dad was hard—for her. It had to be, right? Glancing down at her attire, she knew Danny's shirt highlighted her best assets.

Moved by a compulsion she couldn't ignore, Candy pushed aside the coupons, left the phone untouched, and padded silently down the hallway. The door to his room was open, but the bathroom door was closed. She hesitated outside, slowly squatting down to peek in through the keyhole. Unfortunately, her vantage point revealed nothing except Mr. Olsen's back.

Candy hesitated, unsure what to do. Common sense dictated she should return to the kitchen, order a pizza, and pretend she had never noticed the effect she'd had on him. Another part of her wanted to seize the opportunity, to see if she could spur Mr. Olsen to act on his physical response. Three years of crushing on the man had left her frustrated in more ways than one. Would there ever be another chance again?

As though fate had made the choice for her, Candy swayed in her precarious position just enough to brush against the door, causing it to swing open a few inches. She stared up, feeling exposed and guilty for her spying, as Mr. Olsen came into view. He'd turned toward her, cursing as he reached for the door. He blocked it from opening fully, but there was enough space for her to see what he'd been doing.

His cock jutted from his unzipped pants, glistening with his own arousal. Without thought, she licked her lips, wondering what he would taste like. She had sucked a few cocks the past year, but none had belonged to the object of her long-time youthful lust.

"Candy, what the hell?"

Lifting her gaze to meet his, she asked, "Is that for me, Mr. Olsen?" His cheeks flamed scarlet, and she knew hers must match, judging from how hot they felt.

"I..." He ran a hand through his dark hair, just lightly dusted with gray at the temples. "Why don't you go order the pizza?"

She licked her lips again. "I'm not hungry for pizza, Mr. Olsen."

He groaned, and his cock visibly jerked. "You'd better leave."

Still crouching before him, she asked, "Or what?" It was part challenge, but also part genuine innocence. What would happen if she stayed? She could imagine and hope, but unless she remained glued to the spot, she would never know for sure.

He cursed. "Candy, I'm trying to do the right thing here, but it's hard. I haven't had sex since Becca's mom died. My control isn't that great, and with you sitting there, your mouth so close—" Mr. Olsen broke off with an audible groan.

Tentatively, Candy changed position, to rest on her knees before him. It brought her mouth even closer, and he was easily within touching distance when she reached out a trembling hand to feel his thigh. She stroked the skin with one of her nails, enjoying the crisp spring of hair under her fingers. Perhaps the trembling was contagious, because Mr. Olsen's body quivered under her hand.

She drank in the sight of his full cock, impressed by the size and captivated by the drip of pre-cum hanging from the tip. It seemed suspended in time, defying gravity with impunity. Her attention didn't waver from the drop as she studied it. The focus of her world shrank to that small trickle of arousal, and she leaned forward to intercept it as time suddenly resumed and the dab yielded to the inevitable to cascade from his cock. It was warm on her tongue, a fleeting taste before disappearing.

After one more second, giving Mr. Olsen a chance to protest again, or push her away, Candy leaned closer to put her mouth around the head of his cock. He moaned and stepped closer, surrendering to her seduction as she engulfed the length of him. Her eyes watered as the tip hit the back of her throat, but she refused to give in to the urge to cough or withdraw, sensing any lack of confidence on her part would cause him to break away.

Instead, she followed instinct and began sucking his shaft, slowly rocking back before surging forward again to work the length of him. All the while, she sucked him, wanting more of the elusive drops of pre-cum and teasing them from him a bit at a time. Soon, his flavor bloomed in her mouth and filled her senses. Feeling obsessed, she sucked harder, bringing him in deeper, in her quest to drain every drop of fluid from his rigid cock.

Mr. Olsen wasn't a passive bystander, by any means. He was thrusting into her mouth, his hand twined in her hair to anchor her head against him. She matched his thrusts, taking every bit he offered. As his cock spasmed, she sucked harder, concentrating her efforts on the head as she tongued the sensitive nerves on the underside. With a harsh cry, he released a torrent of satisfaction inside her mouth, offering more than she could take, though she made a valiant effort to swallow every last drop.

She lessened the suction, but held him gently in her mouth as the throbbing in his cock slowly subsided. His hand in her hair slackened, and he began stroking her strands instead of holding her against him. Her heart raced in her ears, and she suddenly became aware of the cinnamon vanilla scent from the air freshener as the focal point of her world expanded to include more than just Mr. Olsen's cock.

As though controlled by an outside force, they moved as one, with her releasing his cock as he stepped back. Pain in her knees made itself known, and she grimaced slightly, hoping he wouldn't see the expression and think he was the cause.

Candy leaned back on her calves, looking up at him through the veil of her lashes, finding the ability to speak crushed by shyness. Perhaps he felt the same, because he didn't say anything. Instead, he just stroked her cheek before offering her a hand so she could get to her feet.

It was the most natural thing in the world to snuggle against him when he enfolded her in a hug. Candy lifted her head to say something, but he intercepted her mouth in a deep kiss that prevented any conversation. The sensual caress of his lips against hers made it hard to think, and she groaned as she snuggled closer. Her head was reeling by the time he broke the kiss, and she followed him in a bit of a stupor as he took her hand, leading her slowly across the hall to his room.

She waited for a sense of panic or uncertainty to grip her as they crossed the threshold into his bedroom, but it never came. This was right. She wanted him, and he definitely wanted her. Becca would never know, so whom would it hurt? No one.

As he paused near the bed, Candy reached for the hem of her shirt, lifting it with shaking hands that impeded the task. By the time she had shed the pale gray cotton and thin pink panties, Mr. Olsen had rid himself of the rest of his clothes as well. His hungry gaze examined her from head to foot, and she resisted the urge to cover her chubby stomach and thighs. From his expression, he found nothing objectionable about her body, and she didn't want to ruin the moment with her own insecurities.

"You're a sexy woman, Candy." He blinked. "When did you become a woman? Why didn't I notice before?"

She shrugged, having no answer.

With another rake of his hand through his hair, Mr. Olsen said, "I want to taste your tits. I'll bet they're even more delicious than they look."

Her cheeks were hot with embarrassment and arousal as she arched her back. He guided her to the bed, where Mr. Olsen sat on the edge and positioned her in front of him, still standing. His mouth was level with her breasts, and she closed her eyes as he leaned forward. His lips were soft and wet as they took possession of one of her large nipples. Sparks of electricity seemed to emanate from the tip when he tongued one. He cupped the other breast in his hand, and she moaned when he tugged gently on the taut bud.

As Mr. Olsen sucked and squeezed her tits, her pussy pulsed in time with the motion of his mouth, weeping fluid that made her thighs slick and had her tightening them in a futile attempt to find relief from the ache building inside. As though he sensed her need, his fingers parted the light dusting of curls shielding her moist folds, seeking out her clit to stroke in time with the movement of his hand on her nipple. "Mr. Olsen," she said in a husky voice, unable to articulate exactly what she wanted.

He paused from sucking her breast just long enough to say, "Gib," before resuming his self-appointed tasks.

"Gib." It was more a breath than a sound. Candy tossed back her head as he slid a finger inside her, while his thumb worked small circles around her clit. His mouth and other hand never ceased, turning her into a pile of sensation, incapable of rational thought. She was vaguely aware of mewls of pleasure escaping her, but was too consumed with need to be self-conscious about the sounds. As her orgasm approached, she arched against him, taking his finger deep inside her. A pinch of pain served to heighten her release instead of diminishing her ecstasy, and Candy cried out as she came hard, her thighs squeezing his hand as her pussy milked his digit.

Lost in a haze of arousal and satiation, Candy collapsed against Gib, allowing him to guide her to the bed, until they were lying side by side. She gazed into his caramel-brown eyes, finding it all too easy to lose herself in the depths.

He placed a chaste kiss on her forehead. "You're sweet, Candy."

She smiled at the silly endearment and the likely unintended pun. "That was amazing, Mr.—Gib."

"Yeah." He exhaled heavily. "I wish this moment never had to end."

She frowned, not liking the note of finality in his tone. "What do you mean?"

"You need to get dressed. Becca will be home soon, and we have to forget this happened."

Candy shook her head. "No. I want to fuck you."

Gib blinked. "You don't mean that."

"The hell I don't." She glared at him. "I've wanted you to fuck me for three years, Gib. I'm not going to suddenly change my mind."

He frowned. "You're a virgin."

She blushed. "How do you know?"

A tender smile curved his lips. "I could feel the resistance when I was fingering you, sweetie."

Her flush deepened. "So what if I am? I'm asking you to change that."

He hesitated, but eventually shook his head. "I can't. It's not for me to be the one. I'm too old, you're too young, and there is no future for us."

Annoyed, Candy sat up. "Don't you care what I want?"

He sighed. "Of course I do, but I know this is a bad idea. You'll realize it too, when you've had time to think it over."

Feeling sulky, and hating the immature emotions welling up in her, Candy took several deep breaths to stave off the urge to cry. "What's so damned important about being a virgin? This is the twenty-first century."

Gib ran a hand through his hair, further tousling it. "I'm not saying you need to wait 'til you're married, but you really will regret it if you give up your cherry in the equivalent of a one-night stand. You'd feel that way whether it's to me or some guy you've just met in a bar."

He was wrong. She knew his words made sense, but they felt wrong on an instinctual level. But looking at his determined face told her he had decided and was going to be noble. Damn him. "Fine, so put it in another way."

With a scowl, he said, "You don't really mean that."

Candy nodded. "I do. I'm not an anal virgin, Gib. I've been in college for a year, you know? It's not a big deal."

His mouth seemed permanently ajar before he managed to close it. "Why in the world would you pick the back way when you could have had sex with any of the guys you've met?"

She shrugged. "I didn't want any of them to be the first. You don't want to be, so I'm offering a compromise."

Gib cursed softly. "I should send you away right now." He shook his head. "This is a bad idea."

"No, it feels good. Probably not as good as your cock in my pussy, but I like it in the backdoor. If that's all I'm going to get from you, I want it."

With a groan, he got off the bed in one motion.

Candy frowned. "What are you doing?"

"Making a complete ass of myself." He gave her a weak grin. "I don't have anything in here, but there's some baby oil in the bathroom. Wait right here."

While he was gone, Candy considered several ways to get him to change his mind, but reluctantly conceded Gib would not be the one to take her virginity. At least, not tonight, she thought with a wicked grin as he returned. She had all summer to wear away his resistance.

She flipped over on her stomach, wriggling into a position that left her ass in the air, cheeks open in offering. Candy squealed at the first splatter of oil as the greasy substance trickled down her buttocks and into her waiting hole. The squeal turned to a moan when Gib began massaging the oil around the puckered bud, slowly parting the sphincter to prepare her for his invasion. First a finger sank into her, before another joined it, as Gib corkscrewed them in and out of her, leaving her loose and welcoming for his thick cock.

Candy grasped handfuls of the coverlet when he cupped her hips, bringing the head of his cock against the relaxed opening. She concentrated on remaining loose as Gib penetrated her, a bit at a time. She lifted her hips, arching back to meet him, as he slid his full length inside her.

She gasped when one of his oiled hands moved around to search between her thighs, finding the needy little clit begging for his touch. His fingers were slippery against the already lubricated bud, soaking wet with her own juices. Candy cried out his name as he finger fucked her while pistoning his hips to enter her back passage as deeply as possible, before withdrawing to plunge into her again. With frantic lifts of her hips, she met his cock and fingers eagerly, eager for another orgasm.

Forcing herself to focus, she gently massaged his cock by clenching her buttocks as she thrust against him, while he continued driving her wild by stroking her clit in rhythmic circles. She came with a small scream, but he continued arching into her, his only concession to her release a lightening of his touch on her clit, to allow for the increased sensitivity. Twice more, Gib made her come before he finally surrendered to his own need, filling her insides with an explosion of cum that made her clench her rear muscles around him in a vain attempt to keep him inside her. Another orgasm stole over her, leaving her gasping, face pressed against the comforter, as tears rolled from her eyes.

At some point, he withdrew from her, joining her on the bed to hold her for an indeterminate time before Candy finally forced herself to return to full awareness. They stared into each other's eyes for a long moment, and she became more determined that sometime in the next few months, before returning to college, Gib would be the one to take her virginity. In the meantime, this was enough. For now.

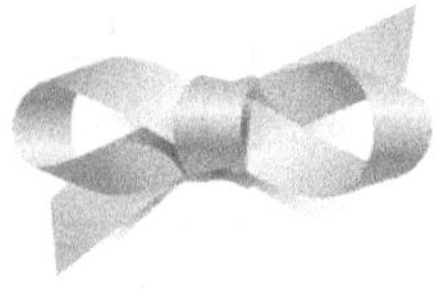

Bonus Excerpt from Kris

IF YOU ENJOYED "SWEET Candy," please continue reading for an excerpt of "Fool No More," also by Kris Kollins.

Michael wants Lori. It doesn't matter that she's 19 and he's 38. He doesn't care that her father is his business partner. He couldn't care less that they're at a cocktail party in his partner's home. All that matters is if she wants him too. And Lori does. Tonight, she's going to show Michael how much.

I followed her into the study where she had disappeared during the peak of her father's party, closing the door quietly behind me, and engaging the lock. I couldn't blame Lori for seeking refuge from the boring business discussions circulating through the opulent house. Due to my partnership with Richard, her father, I had no choice about attending them either, but I preferred to let him handle the schmoozing, while I dealt with the behind-the-scenes business in the office.

As she leaned against the wall, her back to me, I couldn't help admiring the way the red dress clung to her ass, tight and firm, as I expected it to be. At nineteen, attending university on a tennis scholarship, although she had no financial need for one, Lori was lithe and toned, with pert breasts, enough curves to fill any outfit, and ebony hair that fell to her waist when she freed it from the clip binding it currently.

I had wanted her for the past year, ever since I saw her sunbathing by the pool one weekend, a pink bikini molding her curves, with her tits straining to escape the squares of triangles confining them, and realized she was a woman, no longer a little girl. Thirty-seven then, and involved with a woman I was supposed to marry, I tried to push aside my lustful thoughts centered on my friend's daughter.

Tonight, drunk on too much Scotch, and bitter about the passing of the first anniversary of what should have been my wedding to the faithless Anna, I decided to fuck being honorable and go after what I wanted—Lori.

I set the half-empty Scotch on the desk as I passed by it. Her head jerked in my direction with surprise as I bore down on her. "Michael?" I watched her pink lips, outlined with some shiny substance, form my name, and my cock hardened, imagining those lips around my shaft, leaving a glossy pink mark behind.

I didn't give her a chance to turn to face me when I stepped up behind her, pushing her body against the unyielding wall, bringing my hand down to her ass to cup one of her cheeks.

Her voice was fearful, but held more than a trace of excitement. "What are you doing?"

"Touching you." I squeezed her ass in my hand hard enough to make her gasp. My cock jerked in my pants, begging to be freed so it could plunge inside her tight pussy. Would she be a virgin? I didn't care.

"Why?" She trembled under my hand when I slipped it from her ass to the hem of her dress, caressing her thigh, as I slid up the dress.

Available at your favorite ebook vendor

Spanking Stacia

After seeing the large red "F" on her copy of the most recent pop quiz, Stacia was unsurprised when Professor Drake called to her as she tried to exit the college classroom. Stifling a sigh, she trudged over to the podium, where he was stacking papers neatly in a leather satchel. Mr. Drake's hands moved with precision, his long fingers nimbly sorting papers into folders and folders into his bag.

Her thoughts were still on how it might feel to have those same fingers moving across her skin, so it took her a second to realize the professor was speaking.

"You simply have to grasp the basics, Stacia, or you won't be able to understand anything in this class."

Forcing her gaze from his hands to his equally appealing blue eyes, she nodded. "Yes, sir."

"I'd like to see you in my office tomorrow afternoon. I've reserved you a spot for three p.m. Do not be late."

Stacia nodded, mentally checking tomorrow's schedule. She would have to skip a sociology lecture, but her grades were good in that class. Physics 101 was the killer class, and she wasn't foolish enough to reject Professor Drake's offer of assistance.

• • ✺ • •

"I'M TELLING YOU, IT will work. Just try for a few more classes," said Maria before slurping on her milkshake.

Glumly, Stacia dragged a French fry through a pile of ketchup. "It won't. I've dressed sexy for the past few classes." She dipped her head and lowered her voice before adding, "I even wore a short skirt and *no underwear* the day of the pop quiz. I definitely sat high enough that he couldn't miss the fact, but I never saw him even glance my way. Professor Drake doesn't care about how sexy I can look. He wants me to actually know the topics."

It was only fair that she earn the grade by knowing the material, and she couldn't blame the professor for not picking up on her clumsy attempts at seduction. Maria had been the one to suggest the strategy, but she had embraced it—and not to pass the class. She'd never admit it to her roommate and best friend, because Maria thought dating the college professors was gross, but Stacia wanted more than a passing grade from Professor Drake. A lot more. From her visual inspections during class, she would guess at least seven inches more.

"Just try once more. You'll have him all to yourself in his office. Wear a short skirt, a thong, and a low-cut shirt." Maria grinned. "He might have invited you to his office so he can take you up on what you've been offering."

Stacia set down the fry without trying to eat it, her stomach churning with nervous tension. The professor was definitely hot, and the girls flocked around him despite his seeming obliviousness. He was probably in his mid-thirties and must have had experienced lovers. She hardly qualified. With her small breasts and quiet demeanor, no wonder he hadn't noticed her short skirts and flirty shirts. Her wheat-blond hair and light-blue eyes were more farm-girl than stripper. With the exception of one boyfriend last semester, even guys her own age hadn't noticed her, with or without sexy clothes, so why would he?

· · ❧ · ·

STACIA KNOCKED ON PROFESSOR Drake's door four minutes before three p.m. the next day. She might not know anything about physics, but she could impress him with her punctuality. And maybe her state-of-dress? With Maria's badgering, she had chosen a plaid skirt reminiscent of Catholic schoolgirls. The suggested thong was the next piece in her arsenal—though it felt more like it was in her ass. She resisted the urge to dig it out of her crevice. To avoid a total cliché, she had worn a red sleeveless shirt with the navy and red skirt instead of a white button-down.

"Come in."

She opened the door, fighting her inherent shyness. Stacia closed it behind her without being asked and walked toward the desk. She stood in front of him for a long moment as the professor finished the last bite of his apparently late lunch.

"Sit."

She sat, disheartened that his expression didn't change at all when he glanced up at her. For all the awareness he'd given, she might as well be another chair. Stacia crossed her legs, swinging her foot slightly, as Maria had shown her. Paired with lacy white socks, the naughty shoes were deceptively innocent maryjanes, but the platform heel elevated them to something more. They were Maria's, since her sexiest shoes were a pair of open-toed flats.

"Did you take physics in high school, Stacia?" asked Professor Drake. He pushed a strand of black hair off his forehead as he leaned back in the executive chair.

Her gaze flickered to his hand in his hair, but she forced it back to the professor, almost meeting his eyes. "Yes, sir."

"Did you pass?"

She nodded. "Barely," she said in a whisper.

"Yes, I'm sure." He lifted a stack of papers from a tray on his desk. "I've reviewed your work, and you seem to have the most trouble with Newton's Laws of Motion."

She nodded. "I can recite them, but I don't really understand them."

"I've devised a lesson for you. I think it will help you understand the principles."

"Thank you, Professor Drake." She let her gaze sweep his desk, relieved not to find any family photos on display. He didn't wear a wedding ring and had never mentioned having kids, but he must be involved with someone. She was probably a sophisticated woman near his age. No doubt an intellectual, who had never needed a demonstration of Newton's laws.

"Come here, please."

Stacia stood up and walked over to stand beside his desk, where he had indicated.

"Tell me the first law."

"'Every body continues in its state of rest, or of uniform motion in a straight line, unless it is compelled to change that state by forces impressed upon it.'"

Professor Drake nodded. "Tell it to me in another way."

She frowned, struggling to remember. "Oh, yeah. Bodies at rest or in motion tend to stay at rest or in motion unless acted upon by an outside force."

"Very good." He pointed to a large paperweight on his desk. "Would you agree the paperweight is at rest?"

Stacia nodded.

"Pick it up and drop it gently."

She frowned. "But—"

Professor Drake waved at it. "You won't break it."

Stacia lifted the paperweight with caution, surprised at how heavy it was. She brought it about a foot from the floor and dropped it. "Me dropping it was the outside force, right?"

He gave her a hint of a small smile. "Good girl."

She tried not to be too pleased by the faint praise.

"Tell me the second law, and another way to phrase it."

She reeled it off without hesitation, since memorization had never been the problem. "'The acceleration produced by a particular force acting on a body is directly proportional to the magnitude of the force and inversely proportional to the mass of the body.'" Taking a deep breath, she added, "'The acceleration of an object is dependent upon the force acting upon the object and the mass of the object.'" Wringing her hands, she said, "I don't understand that."

The professor nodded. "Pick up the paperweight again." After she had done so, he said, "Throw it down."

Stacia shook her head. "It might break."

"It won't." He sounded impatient.

Eager to avoid his displeasure, she lifted it higher and put some force into dropping the paperweight. This time, it hit the floor, bounced, and rolled over, landing a few feet farther than the first time she had dropped it.

Professor Drake leaned forward slightly. "Do you understand? The speed, or velocity, of the outside force affects how fast or forcefully the object moves."

Blinking, Stacia nodded. "I get it. I mean, I actually understand it, sir."

He rewarded her with another smile. "I'm glad."

She walked over to get the paperweight, returning it to his desk. At his request, she recited the third law. "To every action there is always opposed an equal reaction; or, the mutual actions of two bodies upon each other are always equal, and directed to contrary parts.'"

"Do you understand what that means?"

"I think so. For every action, there is an equal and opposite reaction?"

His smile widened. "That's right. I think a hands-on demonstration is still in order."

"Yes, sir."

"Drop the paperweight again."

With a frown, Stacia did as he asked, wondering how this would be applicable to Newton's Third Law.

"Now, pick it up please."

She bent down to lift it and yelped when he put his arm around her waist. In a second, she found herself on his lap, butt up, and head close to the floor. "What are you doing?" she screeched.

"For the action of running around half-dressed, here is my reaction." His palm slapped against her buttocks with a resounding crack.

Crying out from mingled shock and pain, she struggled to free herself.

The professor continued holding her, seemingly without effort. His hand came down on her cheeks in a precise rhythm, each slap accompanied by the sharp sound of flesh against flesh. Her skin burned and ached under his hand, but her pussy tingled. Was this really turning her on?

After a few more strokes, he stopped, resting his palm across her stinging bottom and rubbing in small circles.

"Are you done?" she asked timidly, voice trembling as she fought to suppress tears. He didn't answer. She heard him rummaging through his desk and braced herself for something else.

"Your action yesterday was sitting in the third row, legs splayed, so I could see you weren't wearing panties."

Her cheeks burned with humiliation, and she made no attempt to deny his charge.

"My reaction is this."

Something thin and painful slapped her bottom. Within a few hits, she had tentatively identified it as a ruler. He uniformly spanked her, alternating cheeks and spots. "Please stop." But did she really want him to? It hurt much worse than his hand, but it felt so good in such a wicked way.

The ruler disappeared, and he rubbed her ass again. "A sore bottom is your reaction to my action."

"I understand now, sir. Please, can we stop the lesson?" To her surprise, he pulled her up, changing her position so that she was lying mostly on her side across his lap, their heads only a few inches apart. Tears streaked down her cheeks, and he leaned forward to lick them away. She shuddered at the contact, her pussy creaming as the sharp pain faded to a duller ache.

He must have decided to ignore her plea to end the lesson. "What is my reaction to having you across my knee, your shapely ass barely covered by that little black thong?"

Stacia shook her head. "I...I don't know, sir."

"Stop calling me sir, or professor. My name is Gideon. Say it." He worded the request in a tone that made it more of a command.

Confused, she said, "Gideon."

He shifted her slightly, so that his cock pressed against her hip. "What is my reaction, Stacia?"

Could her cheeks get any redder? Fighting the blush, she said, "You're hard, sir."

He slapped her on the hip, close to her buttocks. "What's my name?"

"Gideon."

"Good girl. What are you going to do about my throbbing hard cock? What is your reaction to my action?"

Stacia licked her lips as desire coursed through her. "What do you want me to do, Gideon?"

"I want you to fuck me."

"Okay." She sounded so calm, as though this sort of thing happened to her every day. Inside, she was still reeling, trying to process how she had ended up on his knee and then on his lap, her ass stinging and her pussy pulsing.

He assisted her to straddle him, his hand venturing between their bodies to push aside her thong and slip inside her pussy. Gideon chuckled. "Wet. Do you like being spanked, Stacia?"

"I'm not sure."

He pressed a finger inside her dripping cunt. "Really, you aren't sure?"

She closed her eyes as he pushed deep inside her, trying to remember the question. "I'd never thought about it, but I would have thought I didn't."

"What do you think now?" He plunged a second finger into her sheath, pumping them in and out of her with maddening slowness. "Do you like being spanked?"

"Yes, oh, yes, sir." She yelped when he swatted her tender ass with his free hand. "I'm sorry. Gideon."

"Good girl." The professor continued his leisurely exploration, making her writhe and squirm against his hand.

"Please, I want to come."

His reaction was another sharp slap to her buttocks. "When I tell you to, and not before. Do you understand?"

"Yes, Gideon." Why was it so delicious to be submissive to him? And why did she have the urge to provoke him into another spanking? As it was, her butt was so sensitive she didn't know if she would be able to sit on it for hours.

He circled her clit with his thumb, pressing lightly against the hood, while she tried not to move or speak. Her body had a mind of its own, and she couldn't resist the urge to thrust to meet him.

"Now."

"Now?" she asked, dazed and so lost in sensation that she had no idea what he meant.

"Come now, Stacia."

She let loose, almost collapsing under the weight of her release. Her body trembled, and convulsions tightened her pussy. At some point, his fingers left her, and she whimpered in protest, but couldn't find the ability to form words as she surrendered to the onslaught of her orgasm.

As she started to come down from the sexual high, he nudged her thighs farther apart. Stacia's eyes widened when his cock nestled against the entrance to her pussy. He must have freed himself in the time it took her to come.

"Do you want this, Stacia?"

She nodded.

Gideon circled his hips, teasing her. "Say it."

"Please fuck me, Professor Drake."

"Minx." It sounded like a growl. In one motion, he thrust upward while his hands on her hips pulled her down to meet him. His cock overfilled her, making her moan. Her professor was definitely seven inches, and maybe more. The hardest part to take was his girth, but his cock stretched her in a magnificent way. He held her still, not allowing her to move when she tried to ride him. "Say my name."

"Gideon."

His grip slackened, allowing her to arch against him. Gideon set the pace, moving her hips as he thrust upward inside her. Each time he buried himself to the hilt, she cried out, arching downward to rub her clit against his cock through the walls of her cunt. When he commanded her to come, it was like her body had been waiting for permission. Waves of pleasure washed over her as his cock spasmed inside her, filling her with his hot cum. He was breathing as hard as she was, and he seemed to have finally lost a measure of his phenomenal control. Resting her forehead against his, she allowed herself a small smile and a surge of satisfaction, knowing she had made him come undone—literally.

He kissed her cheek, and he cupped her chin to position her mouth for his possession. His tongue swept inside, conquering her, though she offered no resistance. Finally, when she was on the verge of passing out from lack of oxygen, and debating whether she could die happily instead of breaking the kiss, he pulled back.

"What is your reaction to that, Gideon?" she asked with cheeky confidence.

"Spectacular. If you continue to do this well on your lessons, I'm sure you will learn everything you need to know to pass my class on your own merits."

Stacia shifted slightly so she could rub her pussy against his semi-stiff cock, still lodged inside her. "I think I'll learn a lot more than that, sir."

He grinned. "You are just begging for another spanking, Stacia."

With a wicked grin, she said, "I know...*sir*."

• • ❧ • •

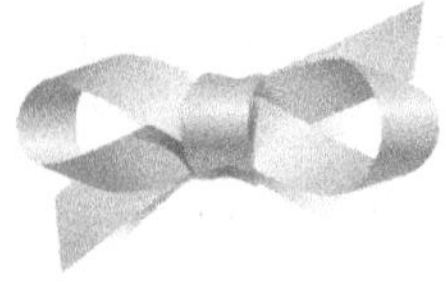

Bonus Excerpt from Tina

IF YOU ENJOYED "SPANKING Stacia," please continue reading for an excerpt of "Silk Scarf Seduction," also by Tina Parker.

Against her better judgment, Tasha accepts a mysterious date with a stranger. They're both wearing masks, and he proceeds to seduce her with the aid of sensual silk scarves. When Tasha finds out the identity of her seducer, she turns the tables on him and puts him at her mercy.

The dress arrived with a cryptic note. Tasha opened the door at the first knock, after the broken doorbell gave a strident peal that faded into a torturous shriek. A UPS driver, wearing a dark brown uniform, handed her a clipboard. "Delivery for T. Greenfield."

"That's me."

"Sign in the electronic box." He indicated the laser pen attached to the clipboard, and Tasha scrawled her name.

She took the large box from him, and he left, whistling *Old Susannah* off-key. Tasha brought the box in the house and closed the door behind her.

After she set the box on the threadbare couch, Tasha searched for a pair of scissors or a box cutter. She settled for a kitchen knife and returned to the box. She carefully opened the tape. She expected to find the wallpaper and carpet samples Linden-Ashby Interiors had promised to send by mid-week. It was already Friday.

Tasha removed the tissue paper and gasped at what lay beneath it. It was a garment of some kind, made of emerald green velvet and satin. Tasha lifted the lid of the box to verify the address.

T. Greenfield
624 Bluegate Rd., Rt. 2

Jackson, Washington

It was supposed to be her package, but she knew it couldn't actually be hers.

Even though she was positive it was a mistake, Tasha lifted out the material. It fell to the floor with a soft whisper, as the velvet slid through her fingers. It was an elegant evening dress, reminiscent of a ball gown from more than a century ago, minus the bustle.

The fitted bodice plunged daringly, and was trimmed with shiny satin in the same shade of green as the dress. The sleeves were tiny caps of wispy lawn, in a paler shade of green. The skirt flared out at the waist, and the hemline was piped with satin. When she turned the dress, Tasha found a discreet zipper at the back.

Very gently, Tasha laid the dress across the worn couch and looked into the box. She hoped to find an explanation. Instead, she found a pair of emerald green kid slippers—just her size, a seven narrow—a long black cloak, and a mask. She lifted the mask from the paper to admire its beauty. It was plain green satin, with tiny seed pearls stitched at the corners of the eyes to imitate feathers. It was a half-mask, meant to cover only from her eyebrows to the bridge of her nose. Satin ribbons extended from the sides, to fasten the mask around her face.

She gave into temptation and lifted the mask over her face before she walked to the cracked mirror in the hallway that had hung there since long before she was born. The mask brightened the hint of green in her brown eyes and minimized her blunt nose. Her mouth appeared full and lush, and the color of the mask was very complimentary with her russet curls.

With a sigh, Tasha removed the mask and laid it beside the dress and slippers, before she delved back into the box. When she found a small cream card, at first she assumed it would have the owner's name listed. Instead, in bold, slashed letters, the note read:

A car will arrive for you at eight this evening, and will wait exactly five minutes. If you don't come out, or if you aren't alone, the car will drive off. The dress and accessories are yours with my compliments, regardless of your decision, Tasha.

There was no signature or clue as to who had sent the note. The sight of her name in the black scrawl sent a frisson of excitement darting through her. The UPS driver had not accidentally delivered this box to her. Clearly, the sender had intended she receive it.

It was probably Kita. Her best friend was notorious for strange gifts and games of intrigue, and Tasha didn't imagine the four hundred miles that now separated her from Portland would keep Kita from her fun. Tasha put the card and dress back in the box, then haphazardly tossed the shoes and mask atop it, before she covered it all with the cloak.

It was a shame the dress would go to waste, but she didn't believe in taking chances. Both times she had done so, it had cost her too dearly. First a broken heart, followed by a ruined career years later.

She returned to the kitchen where she had been cleaning. Tasha replaced the rubber gloves she had removed in her haste to open the door and attacked the years of gunk left on the stove by her disinterested father. She had been at it less than five minutes when she impatiently ripped off the gloves and tossed them aside.

She muttered to herself as she stomped into the living room. Tasha tripped on a hole in the carpet and barely regained her balance. She kicked the spot before she returned to the couch and gently lifted the dress, shoes, and mask from the box. With an impatient sigh, she walked up the creaking stairs and hung the dress in the closet of the room she was using.

Whoever had bought it had obviously spent a large sum, and she didn't want it wrinkled beyond recognition. Tasha wanted to return it in good shape, as soon as she figured out whom to return it to.

Satisfied, Tasha left the master bedroom, which had stood unused for over a year before she moved back to the house. She returned to her chores in the kitchen, but the dress beckoned to her.

If it was a prank by Kita, there was no harm in indulging her friend. She couldn't think of anyone else who would do such a thing, and the thought of wearing the dress was tempting.

Be reasonable, she chided herself. If the person who sent the dress wasn't her friend, they could have any number of motives. It was better to be safe than sorry.

But would she be sorry if she played it safe?

Purchase from your favorite ebook vendor

Also by Kristianna Sawyer

Bad Boys In Blue
Chloe and the Cop
Sera and the Sheriff
Mandy and the Detective

QuikRead
Oh, Baby 3!
Teaching Harper
David's Baby
Guarding Isis
Jesse's Girl
Kaity's Forbidden Fantasy
Loving Lacey
Taking Kylie
Movie Stars' Baby
Having His Baby
Erin's Unexpected Lover
Layla's Birthday Baby
QuikRead Collection

Also by Kris Kollins

Fool No More
Sweet Candy
An Older Man Bundle

Also by Tina Parker

Silk Scarf Seduction
Spanking Stacia
Student Bodies
An Older Man Bundle